Freddy Leon

·

Cat Stories from Lanza

Freddy Leon was born and brought up in Germany but for many years he has lived on the fabulous island of Lanzarote. In the southern town of Playa Blanca he cares daily for the wellbeing of the many stray cats who have won his affection.

FREDDY LEON

Cat Stories
from Lanzarote

Many humorous stories about, with and by cats

© 2017 Freddy Leon
Type setting and layout: Buch&media Ltd, Munich
Cover design with photograph by © bortnikau, fotolia.com
All illustrations in the text are by Ramona Meili, Switzerland
Translation: Jane Cooper
Produced and published by BoD – Books on Demand
ISBN 978-3-7448–4464-2

Once upon a time …

That's how most fairy stories begin.
But these stories have a background in truth.

Content

Came to stay 9

Arrival. 11

The little bird with the sun hat. 25

A new friend 28

The coach tour. 34

The stroller. 38

Miaow, miaow. Rin the cat's poem 40

Rin the cat (the soft, cosy fur coat). 42

The blue ball 44

Donna and Bella the two siamese cats. 46

Came to stay

Lanzarote – a mystical, unbelievably beautiful island in the Atlantic Ocean. Freddy must have thought that when he came here for the first time. The tourists who come back every year think that too. For me, Lanzarote is a second home. But it also has another side … If you walk along the promenade in the evening you will notice that there are many cats there waiting for something …

Freddy came to Lanzarote in 1994 and stayed. It was hard going in the beginning but he never gave up and he discovered his love for the cats. In those days an old lady used to look after the animals on the beach. When illness forced her to leave the island, she asked Freddy to take care of the cats. That was the start of 'Freddy's Cathouse'. To this day he is still caring selflessly for the wild cats and knows each one by name. There are always more newcomers … the word has gone round that you can be well looked after here.

Freddy has achieved so much in Playa Blanca and we, the 'cat-friends', are very grateful to him for his tireless commitment. Freddy needs every bit of support and gratefully accepts all help. In the meantime permission was granted to set up some nice feeding stations which have been lovingly handcrafted by German cat-friends. Many holidaymakers come and feed the cats in these stations during their stay on the island and are rewarded with wonderful memories to take home. Sometimes they even take home one of their favourites. We know them all: Marylin, Tiger, Tiger 2, Debbie, Dana, Fin und Fefe, the Fluffies, Clare, Miranda (who turned out to be Mirando), Luisa, Oskar, Little Dotty, the Dolly and Daisy family, and of course Prince. And not forgetting all the little pussies that are now no longer with us. Thanks to Freddy they all had a future.

We can't save the world but we can secure the future of the cats in Playa Blanca. Even small gifts are welcome, as apart from food, the cats also need veterinary attention and neutering. I got to know Freddy as a warm-hearted and unbelievably dedicated person. Always indefatigably on the go for the sake of the cats, day in, day out. With the help of my pictures and stories my son compiled a book as a memento of Playa Blanca, and captured my thoughts in these wonderfully poignant words:

The impressions that I collected
are the work of a wonderful person
whose own life wasn't always easy.
Now he has found his destiny:
He is the 'Catfather'

Thank you for your splendid work. Over the years Freddy has gone through a lot with his animals and if cats could write these would prob-ably be their stories … Sometimes funny, sometimes thoughtful; many a two-legged individual will recognise a bit of themselves in the stories. With this book the reader can always have with them a small part of Freddy's cats from Playa Blanca …

Carmen Wegele, Deutschland

Arrival

Once upon a time off the West African coast in the Atlantic Ocean lay a wonderful island in the Canaries called Lanzarote, which is the closest you can get to Paradise …

It was a pleasant summer's day when a large cruise ship coming from Europe (actually it was from Germany if I remember rightly) docked in Lanzarote's harbour.

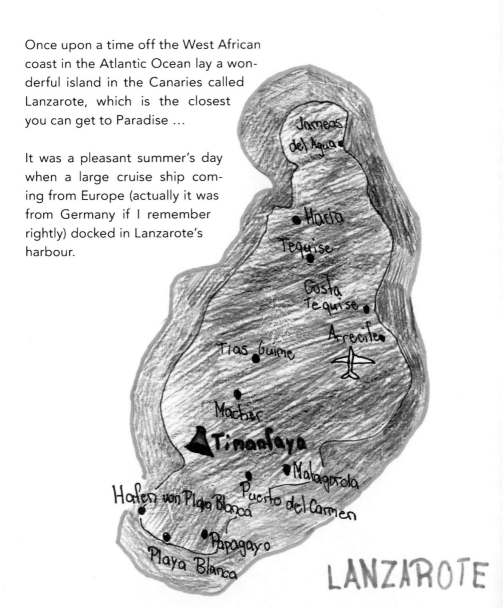

There were numerous passengers on board and some of them left the ship to explore the island's capital, Arrecife. In all the hubbub and activity no one noticed that two cats had also left the ship on their silent velvet paws. Cinderella and Bertolino first hid behind a lorry so that they could get a better look at the many two-legged creatures around them.

They hoped to find someone who was throwing away some food. Cinderella and Bertolino were in the grip of a mega cat-hunger, because it was now several hours since they had hoovered up all the leftover fish and other food they could find on board. They were not in luck. Now they were starving and Bertolino already had tummy ache. Cinderella looked at her friend sympathetically and said "miaow, miaow! You stay here in hiding, Bertolino, and I'll go and have a look round the neighbourhood. Perhaps I can find a delicious morsel for us in a dustbin somewhere. Miaow, miaow!"

And with these words, the black and white cat disappeared. Bertolino, who hated being left on his own, pressed himself close against the lorry tyre and dozed off.

He was woken up by the loud tooting of car horns and shouts emanating from two wildly gesticulating elderly ladies. Through his half-open eyes he could dimly make out his friend picking her way through traffic to his hide-out. Bertolino was enormously pleased to see Cinderella coming back with a big fat chicken bone between her teeth. It was a delicious snack at just the right time.

"Come on, Bertolino", miaowed Cinderella impatiently to her friend who had long since polished off his piece of meat and was still licking his lips. Together they went on their way because they also wanted to have a look round the town. Near the park they met a mummy cat who had just had three kittens. This mummy cat was very proud of her children and told Cinderella and Bertolino: "Miaow, miaow! I only named my little velvet-pawed babies a few days ago." One kitten was snow white except for a few little black spots on his left paw: he had been given the name 'Snowflake'. The other was completely black and had inspired the name 'Charcoal'. It was funny to watch the little kittens tumbling around. But then there was the third kitten. "Miaow, miaow", sighed the mummy cat. "I can't find a suitable name for my third baby."

"Why not?" asked Bertolino. Instead of the mummy cat, Cinderella piped up: "miaow, miaow … probably because the kitten's coat has a very strange colour." "What nonsense", Bertolino shook his head. "Just call it 'Baby'!" And now that all the kittens had names – of course only thanks to Bertolino's help – the cats said goodbye to each other.

The clock on the tall church in the centre of Arrecife was just striking the hour when Cinderella and Bertolino reached it. Now they had to decide whether they wanted to stay on the island or return to the harbour and travel on with the ship which would be putting out to sea again in an hour's time. They both looked around them and saw the splendid palm trees, cacti and flowers in bloom. Cinderella miaowed: "it's so beautiful here, please let's stay on this island!" "I'd like nothing better," answered Bertolino.

They walked on and a few minutes later found a place to sit down under a date palm. Cinderella had the idea of telling Bertolino a little story.

"Miaow, miaow ... this is a story about three dwarves. Every morning three hard-working dwarves, Pitty, Patty and Rocky, go to work. They have to walk a long way to reach the sandy beaches where they look for valuable olive stones. One warm day, a very, very warm day, as it turned out, the three dwarves found a little cat on their way to work. "What's happened here?" asked Pitty. "What's happened here?" wondered Patty. Then Rocky said "Can we help?" Full of hope the kitten looked up at the three small dwarves and groaned: "Oh, look here, I've cut my paw on a sharp stone and it's badly swollen. Help me please."

The dwarves were just the right people to ask for help. "Of course!" said Pitty. "We'd love to help", nodded Patty in agreement. And Rocky said "I know what to do!" Rocky quickly explained his plan to his dwarf friends. "First we'll make a stretcher for the kitten!" Pitty, Patty and Rocky worked fast and efficiently. In the twinkling of an eye they had built a stretcher. "Now we'll carry you to your parents!" cried Pitty.

The dwarves helped the little cat onto the stretcher and carried her to her cat parents who lived in a garden on the edge of the town. "Miaow, miaooooow, miaooooooooooow" went the cries of the little injured kitten. When her mummy and daddy cats, Roberta and Carlos heard that they ran up to the four of them. Tears of pain rolled down the kitten's face but they were also tears of joy at being reunited with her mummy and daddy cat. "Miaow, miaow … thank you so much dear dwarves for your help!" said the daddy cat. Mummy cat gave Pitty, Patty and Rocky each a kiss for she was overjoyed at the return of her darling little kitten.

Cinderella hadn't noticed that our little cat Bertolino had fallen fast asleep while she was telling the story of the three dwarves. But she was tired too and so they slept side by side dreaming under the date palm until the next morning.

Shortly after dawn, the little velvet-pawed cats had a wash and went on their way. Bertolino and Cinderella left the town. They wanted to find a nice little place of their own. On the edge of a small village they met a family of cats living under a cactus. The old daddy cat and his wife, the mummy cat, were very happy and contented because – as they explained – all their children were married and had cat families of their own.

But this couple themselves had more tiny kittens – a girl and two boys. One of these was called Paul – he was cheeky and impudent. The kittens played hide and seek and tag during the day. In the evening when the sun went down and it got cooler, they crept inside their 'cat house' and kept each other warm until they fell asleep. Then they dreamed about chicken and tuna and sometimes one of the young kittens would even chew or lick his lips in his sleep. But Paul never dreamed about titbits: he dreamed about a little bird.

The little bird with the sun hat

Mummy and Daddy Bird already had a lot of children and yet it was always a great pleasure when the eggshells slowly broke open and the little ones slipped out. And today everyone was very excited … Noises could be heard coming from inside the eggs. At the end just one egg remained. Mummy and Daddy Bird hopped around it feeling puzzled. They looked at it from all angles:

   "What's wrong with that one, peep, peep?" Daddy Bird asked his wife. "Should we help out somehow?"

   "Perhaps the shell is too thick and our baby can't break through it?" twittered Mummy Bird and looked perplexed at her husband.

"It's OK, all's well. I get it" replied Daddy Bird as he began to gently tap around the egg with his beak. Mummy Bird helped him and then the eggshell finally cracked open.

"But what's this?" tweeted Mummy Bird to her husband. They both looked in astonishment at a little baby chick with a sun hat on its head. The parents eyed one another and shook their little heads in amazement, but also with great pleasure at seeing this extraordinary baby bird.

Paul, our young cat who had dreamt this story, woke up. The dream of the little baby bird had awoken pangs of hunger and the little cat rushed off to gobble down the remains of his supper.

But what has become of the newest inhabitants of Lanzarote, Cinderella and Bertolino? How are they? They had said goodbye to the cat family who lived under the old cactus and were off again in search of a new home. They were very, very lucky. They found themselves a fabulous home near the village restaurant: it was an old abandoned dog kennel all made of wood. Well actually there was a small hole in the roof, but that wasn't a big problem; and anyway it hardly ever rains in Lanzarote. And so they lived – as the fairy tale goes – happy ever after.

A new friend

Rin, Tin and Tan, three little cats, woke up almost together:

the dustbin men were emptying the bins and had woken up the cats with all their crashing and banging. Every morning, except for Sundays, of course, the bin men emptied the bins which were overflowing with plastic bottles, paper, and food waste etc.

A whole load of rubbish was collected not only along the coast road in Playa Blanca (that's what the town in the south of Lanzarote is called), but also in the numerous hotels and trailer parks. It couldn't be long until dawn now. Our three little velvet-pawed friends Rin, Tin and Tan, were feeling – what could be more natural – extremely hungry.

"Miaow, miaow," cried Tan. "Come on, let's go and look for some delicious food for breakfast!" Rin and Tin followed Tan over the terrace of the 'Hesperia Playa Dorada' Hotel in the direction of the cat feeding station in the garden at the back. Quite obviously Freddy Leon (the big two-legged cat friend) hadn't come yet, for the water and food bowls were empty.

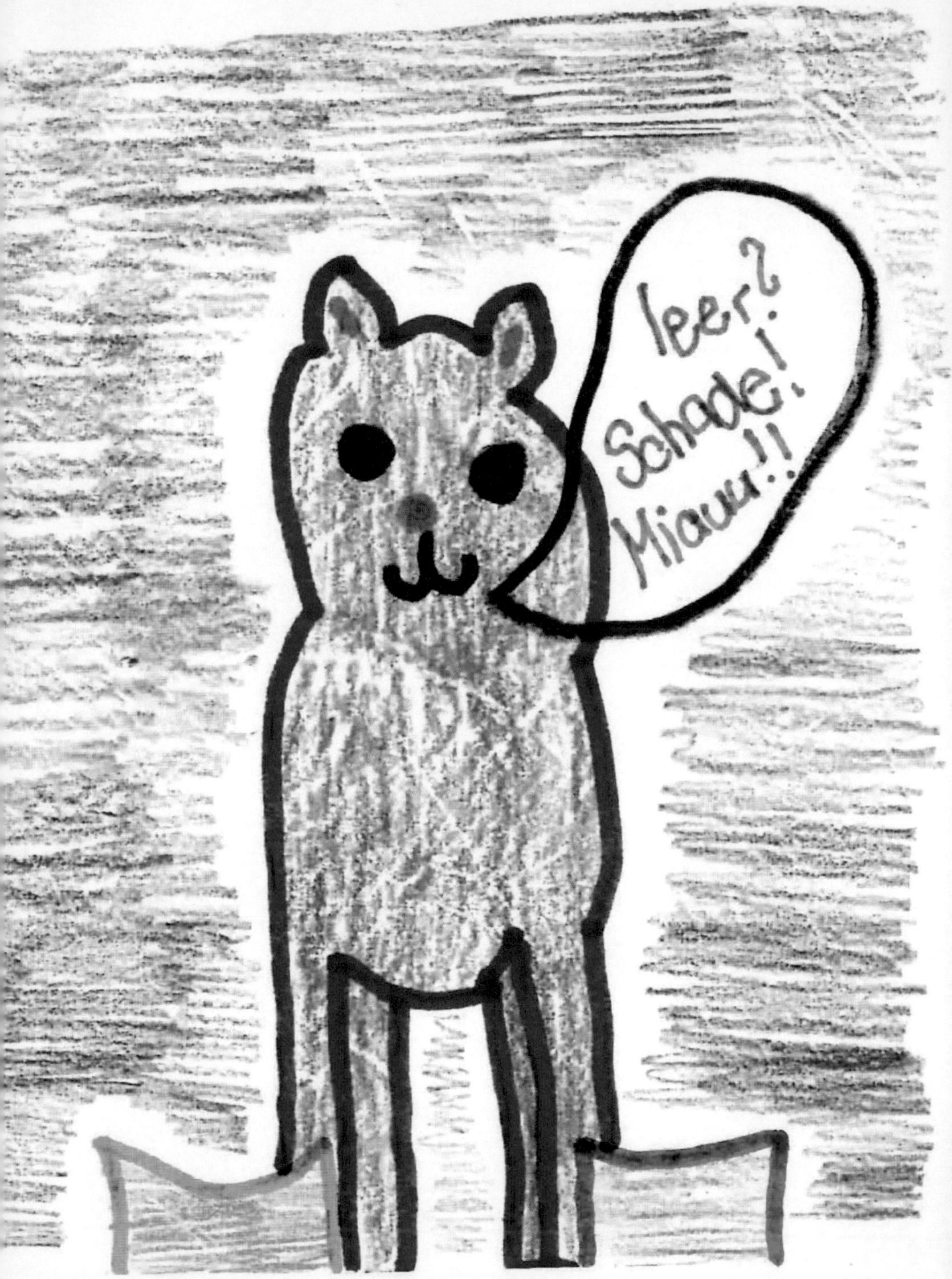
leer?
Schade!
Miauu!!

"Well, let's go on then!" growled Rin. The three cats walked on to the feeding station at the salt mill. There was still fresh water in a bowl there and Tin also found a few snacks of dried food so he made a little breakfast of that.

"Miaow, miaow … follow me to the station on the bridge," commanded Tan, "we'll surely get some breakfast there". A few minutes later three little hungry mouths reached the next feeding station that was known to many cats by the name of 'Freddy's cat house'.

But who was that moving about among the bowls?

"Hey, you there … that's our food!" cried Rin outraged.

"Miaow, get away … miaow, miaow!" cried Tan.

"Be quiet, miaow, it's only a mouse", Tin tried to calm his brother. The tiny mouse was standing on its back legs and squeaked: "It's only me … Yolanda Mouse is my name, and I'm hungry!" she said in her own defence.

The cats had eyed up the little mouse with mistrust, but now they raffled themselves up and introduced themselves to the little interloper. Normally mice are terrified of cats. But Yolanda Mouse was confident and friendly to the three young cats. She stretched out her right paw to shake hands with the cats. Rin, Tin and Tan answered in unison: "Miaow, miaow … Good morning to you, Yolanda Mouse." They made friends and enjoyed a fabulous breakfast together. The tourists who passed the animals on their way to the beach or the town were delighted to see the four cute little animals getting on so well together.

The coach tour

On this particular Sunday five coaches were waiting in the port of Playa Blanca to take the many tourists to the farmers' market in Teguise.

Our three little four-legged friends – you already know their names: Rin, Tin and Tan – had spent the night near the port. Now that they'd eaten a good breakfast at 'Freddy's Cat House', they were lying in the shade under a parked car. They were watching a German family whom they had noticed and Rin purred: "Miaow, miaow … keep quiet. The old man there is telling the little girl a story. Let's listen …"

Our little tigers pricked up their ears to listen to the following story:

"When I was little", began Grandpa Eric, "there weren't as many cars as there are now; they looked completely different and they didn't go as fast. And there weren't any nice comfortable coaches then either. I also remember that my mother and father never went out without their hat and gloves. Our kitchen was very big but we didn't have a dishwasher or a microwave, and there was no central heating either. Yes, I can still remember exactly how the hob and all the saucepans used to sparkle and shine. I grew up on a farm, but my parents didn't have a tractor or a combine-harvester: all the hard work had to be done by hand. We didn't have any holidays like you have today, dear little Wiebke" – for that was the little girl's name – "in those days it was fashionable to have pale skin. People protected their skin with a straw sun hat. And the toys that you have … I mean your play station and even your mobile … hadn't been invented then. We used to love playing marbles and all the girls in the neighbourhood had pretty dolls with real hair."

"How lucky you were, Grandpa, to have lived in those times. It was all so much nicer than it is today," enthused his little granddaughter Wiebke with huge sparkling eyes.

At that moment the doors of the coach opened and Rin, Tin and Tan watched the tourists, including Grandpa and Wiebke get on.

Carefully, and unnoticed, the three little cats slid towards the coachin which Wiebke and her grandfather had disappeared.

"Miaow, we must be careful and quiet, miaow!" Tan warned.

"Should we get on too?" wondered Tin. Rin was ready to jump aboard the coach and gave the order: "now, in you go!"

The doors closed and the coach set off. A coach tour was quite a novelty and very exciting for our little friends. They crept under the back seat.

Tin said in a nervous whisper: "So what shall we do now, miaow?" Tan purred back: "Lie down quietly and enjoy the coach trip!"

Then they heard the grandfather's familiar voice telling his granddaughter some more stories about his childhood. But they couldn't make out the exact words over the noise of engine. Rin, Tin and Tan enjoyed the gentle swaying and the pleasant vibration of the coach under their bodies.

Over an hour later the coach stopped. The doors opened and our three little friends jumped out and sought shade under a cactus.

The courier got out too and tried to tell the group of curious tourists running hither and thither about the departure time:

"Please be back at the coach in good time for the return trip. We leave from the car park here at four o'clock. I wish you all a pleasant time in Teguise. Enjoy the market! See you later!"

The stroller

Dear animal lovers, may I introduce myself? I'm a tomcat. My name is "Fauchi" and I live in Playa Blanca on the Canarian island of Lanzarote. Five other cats are purring and miaowing alongside me in the shelter. Their names are Rin, Mikki, Annabello, Donner and "Mr Baker" – a wise old Siamese and Persian cross-breed cat. For months now we've managed to get a person to provide us with fresh water and food on a daily basis. This person, he's only got two paws, although they are big ones – goes by the name of Freddy and he really loves us cats. That means he doesn't only feed us, he plays with us, cuddles and strokes us regular, and we feel okay in his company.

There are six furry friends sharing this house in an estate, and many other cats have found a place to eat and sleep in the neighbourhood. I often stroll up and down and round about my territory. I like visiting the neighbours. We play hide and seek and enjoy the fabulous weather here. It's like a beautiful dream to lie under the palms and cacti and warm your fur in the sunshine. I often doze off and dream of tasty morsels or big tins of tuna.

A few days ago on one of my strolls I noticed a really sweet and still very young black and white cat. She was trying to jump up onto a wall to eat the food lying on top of it. It was funny to see how often the little kitty had to take a run up to finally get up on the wall. There she enjoyed crunching up the dry food the "cat friends" had left behind. With great pleasure she also gulped down the water that was in a little bowl.

I alerted the black and white kitten's attention to my presence with a loud hiss. "Miaow, miaooooow! Why are you straying round here and disturbing my meal? What do you want from me?"

I answered: "Miaow, miaooooow! My name is Fauchi and this is my territory, got it? Miaow."

I'd obviously hissed too loudly at the sweet little kitten because she suddenly looked frightened and was about to run away. So I purred softly: "Miaow … I've been watching you for some time and I like the look of you! Shall we take a stroll together through my territory?"

The little black and white one agreed. We trotted round together for several hours. I introduced her to some of my cat friends, miaow, miaow, because I was just a little bit proud to be going out with such a good-looking girl cat. It was a long time after dusk that we said goodbye to one other and of course we agreed to meet again the next day.

Today, many months later, the sweet little cat (I shan't give away her name) has become my best girl. We meet up as often as we can and play with together. Just great! I love my life as a tomcat!

Miaow, miaow. Rin the cat's poem

I'm Rin the cat and I'm feeling so sad
'Cos it's autumn now and the weather is bad
When Freddy comes here with the food today
I might feel more like going out to play.
Slowly his hand comes to stroke my fur
But please be careful – my ear is so sore
The kitchen door opens: I go out in the rain,
But what choice have I got: I can't stay in again!
So I'm following Freddy to see what he's got
And wishing to goodness this rain would just stop.
I lift up my head and stop dreaming like that
I can do it, you see, even though I'm a cat.
Now the rain comes down like a bucket of water
And I'm getting wetter, although I ought not to.
A car goes by and drives straight through the puddle
Soaking my coat – oh, I'm in such a muddle –

"I wanna go home!" I miaow to Freddy
But he's in a bad mood and he isn't ready
To go yet. Oh miaow, I'd give all that I've got
For a dry place to sleep in a nice sunny plot.
But at last we get home and my ordeal is over
My face says I'm fed up, I need a warm cover!
But then Freddy picks me up in his arms
And gives me the chance to go in and get warm,
He rubs me dry and he gives me a kiss
Then a plate of cat food – oh what bliss!
Peter, our friend's come to visit, you see,
He strokes my fur, makes a big fuss of me –
So now the humans are all in my power
And I call that a happy-cat hour.

Rin the cat (the soft, cosy fur coat)

Rin the cat couldn't get to sleep last night. There were too many tourists walking about near his cat house. "I'm lucky that I'm a cat and have a soft and cosy fur coat," he thought. "I can lie down and sleep anywhere."

"Huh, what was that noise?" Rin stood up and listened. The noise came from a hedgehog who was snuffling around close to where Rin had chosen to sleep under an oleander bush.

"You should look for a nice little soft cosy place of your own" Rin called to him. "I've got a soft and cosy fur coat already so I can sleep anywhere. But you've got spikes so you have to find the right place to sleep first." Rin was proud of the sound advice he'd given Antonio the hedgehog, and added: "Sleep tight dear hedgehog. Sweet dreams!"

"Rin's right", thought Antonio the hedgehog. "I'll find myself a soft and cosy little place." He must have said his thoughts aloud, as Oliver the brown and white dog who was just going by asked: "what do you want a soft and cosy little place for?"

"To sleep", Antonio answered and told Oliver the dog what Rin the cat had said.

"That's a good idea," said Oliver, "I'll help you. As a matter of fact I've a cosy fur coat of my own, but at the end of the day you can never have too soft a bed."

Antonio the hedgehog and Oliver the dog were barely underway when they met Cindy the Swan. "Hallo, Miss Swan, could you help us please?" said Oliver, "we're looking for a soft and cosy little place." They told the majestic bird about the advice Rin the cat had given Antonio the hedgehog.

"That's a fantastic idea", gabbled Cindy the swan, "and I've got time to help you search."

In the meantime, Rin the cat had just settled down comfortably in his bed, when suddenly he heard a loud crack. "What's going on in the hotel garden today? It's very noisy." But even the racket in the hotel garden didn't stop Rin from dropping off to sleep.

When Rin the cat woke up late in the afternoon he felt very strange as if something wasn't quite right. When he opened his eyes he saw what it was: Antonio the hedgehog, Oliver the dog and Cindy the swan had all lain down to sleep and cuddled up to him.

"Miaow, miaow … Hi you guys!" he laughed.

"Hi", answered Antonio rather embarrassed. "You're probably wondering what we're doing here … But I told the others what you said and we thought it was excellent advice, but it's not easy to find the right place with all these tourists about. Then I remembered how you'd said how soft your fur coat was and so we thought we'd make our bed on you! It really was comfy!"

"Wonderfully soft and cosy and warm," piped up Oliver the dog.

"Miaow, miaow … thanks guys!" purred Rin.

"And now that we've all had such a nice sleep let's eat together," gabbled Cindy the swan.

"Yes," said Rin, "but only if it's fish in white wine sauce!" That was particularly important to him.

The blue ball

The rain had stopped and the many flowers and plants here in Haria, in the valley of a thousand palm trees on Lanzarote, shook themselves with pleasure to be once again showing their best sides. The sun was peeping out through the remaining rain clouds and it was getting pleasantly warm.

A ray of sunshine tickled Mikki and Annabel on the nose. "Atishoo, Miaow! Atishoo, Miaow!" rang out twice, as both kittens awoke from their siesta.

"The sun's back" meowed Annabell.
"What's up?" asked Mikki, still dozy through half-open eyes. "You're a cat, you can feel the sunshine, miaow!" Annabell purred. "Just look what the rain's done." Mikki looked around the neighbourhood and saw how clean the rain had washed the streets and houses after the recent sandstorm. The sleepy little cat could also see the cacti, palm trees, bushes and flowers shaking off the last droplets of rain and stretching themselves.

"Oh, just look over there – that really looks super", Mikki purred, and pointed to the nearest date palms. "The flower over there is extraordinarily blue." Annabel laughed. "You're asleep and still dreaming ... That's not a flower: that's a blue bullet!"

So Mikki the cat set himself the task of finding out what the twinkling blue light under the palm tree was. He was rather a nosey fellow. "Miaow, miaow!" cried Mikki: "that's a blue ball not a bullet!" He gave the ball a hard shove so that it rolled directly to Annabell's feet. Quick as a flash Annabell the kitten lay down on her side and grabbed the ball with her outstretched paw. She gave it a mighty kick with her paw and the ball rolled back to Mikki. It was cute to see the two little velvet paws passing the ball to one other. Suddenly a little voice piped up: "Can I play?"

"Who on earth was that?" asked Annabell.

"Oh look over there – Yolanda the mouse is sitting on a stone!" cried Mikki. True enough, there sat a small grey mouse with a black patch on her back and a cute little straw hat on her head.

"Oh, please, please let me play too," squeaked Yolanda again. But the two little pussy cats didn't want the mouse to play ball with them. They had a totally different thought in their minds when they spotted the mouse, and Mikki the cat warned her: "Get lost, or we'll catch you and eat you up!"

When she heard these words, Yolanda the mouse fled and disappeared down the nearest mouse hole.

Mikki and Annabell went on playing with the blue ball for almost another hour before they lost interest and left it behind in a field of potatoes. Our two little cats suddenly felt rather hungry after their game and made their way towards Haria to look in the large bins there for something to eat.

Donna and Bella the two siamese cats

On Lanzarote there are not only black stones and volcanoes but also fabulously beautiful sandy beaches. Two Siamese cats called Bella and Donna were particularly fond of the natural beaches in Papagayo Park. They liked tumbling around on the fine sand to the sound of the Atlantic waves breaking in the background. Best of all, Donna and Bella liked to lie in little sand hollows and soak up the sunshine. Just like today. After sunbathing the two little cats were hungry and wanted to go home. They'd almost reached the Papagayo Arena Hotel when something stopped them in their tracks. They couldn't go on no matter how hard they tried. Horrified, they realised that they had got caught up in an old fishing net. At that moment there was a strong tug and the net was lifted up in the air together with our two sweet little furry friends Donna and Bella. They could just about make out two boys who were throwing the net into a huge waste bin. Donna and Bella were trembling with fear. It was pitch black all around them. They couldn't see the two boys but they could hear them laughing loudly. It seemed an eternity before they could hear any more faint sounds around them.

"Miaow, miaooow!" complained Bella anxiously. "What's happened to us, miaow?"

Donna answered: "I think we're really in trouble now. Miaow! How are we going to get out of this one?"

The little cats tried to find their bearings in the dark bin. The net lay on a pile of stinking rubbish and the bin lid pressed down on their little bodies. Donna, the braver of the two said in a determined voice:

"Miaow, at least we're still alive, that's the main thing, and someone's bound to find us and get us out of here. Just keep calm, miaow!"

Late in the afternoon the two cats heard people's voices. They stayed quite still, hoping that they were tourists who were going to throw rubbish in the bin. They guessed right! Suddenly it was light again as some-one lifted the lid off the bin.

"Miaow, miaooow, miaoooooooooww!" cried Donna and Bella. Two girls peered down into the container. Of course, they'd heard the cat-erwauling. They freed the two little cats and held them gently in their arms. They stroked and cuddled Donna and Bella and the two cats were thrilled to be free again. They thanked their rescuers with loud purrs and "miaow, miaooows!" Then they ran off in the direction of the Papagayo Arena Hotel.

They reached the "Freddy's Cathouse" cat feeding station where the bowls had just been filled with food and water. Donna and Bella quenched their thirst with cool fresh water and ate until they were full up. "Miaow, miaow miaow … At long last we can recover from the stress and relax", said Donna. They lay down under a wild oleander bush, snuggled up together and soon fell fast asleep out of sheer exhaustion.

Are these cat stories true or have I made them up? You can find out, dear read-ers, by visiting me on my website www.freddyscathouse.weebly.com

Freddy Leon, Playa Blanca, Lanzarote